MW01050663

WITHDRAWN FROM
HERRICK DISTRICT LIBRARY

THE WORLD OF NASCAR

Talkin' NASCAR

By Bob Woods

HERRICK DISTRICT LIBRARY
300 S. River Avenue
Holland, MI 49423

OCT 2 9 2008

The Child's World
www.childsworld.com

The
Child's
World®
www.childsworld.com

Published in the United States of America by
The Child's World®
1980 Lookout Drive • Mankato, MN 56003-1705
800-599-READ • www.childsworld.com

ACKNOWLEDGMENTS

The Child's World®:
Mary Berendes, Publishing Director

Produced by Shoreline Publishing Group LLC
President / Editorial Director: James Buckley, Jr.
Designer: Tom Carling, carlingdesign.com
Assistant Editor: Jim Gigliotti

Photo Credits:
Cover: Joe Robbins
Interior: AP/Wide World: 9, 10; Corbis: 6;
Reuters: 28; Joe Robbins: 1, 2, 4, 12, 15, 17, 18,
21, 22, 25, 26.

Copyright © 2009 by The Child's World®
All rights reserved. No part of this book may be
reproduced or utilized in any form or by any means
without written permission from the publisher.

**LIBRARY OF CONGRESS
CATALOGING-IN-PUBLICATION DATA**

Woods, Bob.
  Talkin' NASCAR / by Bob Woods.
    p. cm. — (World of NASCAR)
  Includes bibliographical references and index.
  ISBN 978-1-60253-081-2 (library bound : alk.
paper)
  1. Stock car racing—Juvenile literature. 2. Stock
car racing—Terminology—Juvenile literature. 3.
NASCAR (Association)—Juvenile literature. I. Title.
II. Series.

GV1029.9.S74W684 2008
796.72—dc22

2008004376

Contents

CHAPTER 1
4 **From Axle to Zoom!**

CHAPTER 2
6 **Car Talk**

CHAPTER 3
12 **Track Terms**

CHAPTER 4
18 **Pre-race Chatter**

CHAPTER 5
24 **Race Rap**

29 **TALKIN' MORE NASCAR**
30 **GLOSSARY**
31 **FIND OUT MORE**
32 **INDEX AND ABOUT THE AUTHOR**

[OPPOSITE]
*Pit road . . . gas 'n' go . . . jack man . . . got
loose—do you know what all these terms
mean? Learn to "talk the talk" inside!*

From Axle to Zoom!

NASCAR HAS ITS OWN SPECIAL LANGUAGE.

It's still good-old English, but to be a true NASCAR fan, you should learn to speak like your favorite drivers. You'll understand him when he says his stock car is either *loose* or *tight*. You'll know that *marbles* on the racetrack aren't something kids play with. You'll be able to tell the difference between a *crankshaft* and a *driveshaft*.

NASCAR has lots of **technical** terms to describe parts of a race car, inside and out. From the *pistons* in the engine to the *axles* connecting the wheels, every part is important.

[OPPOSITE]
After "tradin' paint" with his opponents and grabbing the checkered flag, Jeff Gordon celebrates in Victory Lane.

Like other sports, NASCAR has teams. Each member of the team has a specific title and job. The driver drives, of course. But what about the *crew chief*, the *catch can man*, and the *spotter*? What do they do?

In the days leading up to a race, the driver needs to *qualify* and get a *pole position.* Once the race is underway, drivers look for the best *groove* on the track. On the radio, they talk about things like *drafting*, *slingshot passes*, and *trading paint*. Not until the final lap, however, will one driver enter *Victory Lane*.

Those words may be confusing now. But once you get the hang of NASCAR language, speaking like a NASCAR racer will be as easy as A-B-C.

Car Talk

THERE WOULD BE NO NASCAR WITHOUT STOCK CARS.
So it makes sense to start by learning all about those
colorful, four-wheeled racing machines.

First, *stock* actually has many different meanings.
Although it also can be used to talk about soup, cattle, or
owning part of a company, a car is "stock" when it rolls
out of the factory, shiny and new. No changes are made
to it. Every car is the same.

Way back in the 1930s, daring young men (and
some women) started racing each other in their stock
cars. Before long, stock car racing became a popular sport
in the Carolinas, Georgia, and other states in the South.

The key word in any type of racing is speed. Whether
on foot, horseback, bobsled, or stock car, the winner goes
faster than everyone else. The need for more speed led
those early stock-car drivers to begin *modifying*—which
means changing—their cars. They made the engines
more powerful. They made the cars steer better on the
rough, oval-shaped dirt tracks where races were run.

[OPPOSITE]
*Early NASCAR racers
were just like the cars
people drove to town
or to work . . . except
that most people
didn't try to race!*

They were still called stock cars, and they looked stock, but soon no two were exactly alike.

Today's NASCAR race cars are definitely not stock. Four different companies make cars for NASCAR's Sprint Cup Series. The four models are: Chevrolet Impala SS, Dodge Charger, Ford Fusion, and Toyota Camry.

Other than the names, the *production models* of those cars are nothing like the ones on racetracks. Production models are the cars that manufacturers sell

What NASCAR Means

During the early years of stock car racing, there were very few rules, so some races weren't fair. One driver, William "Big Bill" France, decided to fix that problem. In late 1947, he held a meeting with a group of race organizers. Big Bill—he stood 6 feet, 5 inches tall—suggested starting a new **association** that would organize races and make strict rules for every driver. They agreed, and in 1948 he started NASCAR, the National Association for Stock Car Auto Racing.

Today, NASCAR has three major series:

➤ Sprint Cup: The "major leagues" of NASCAR is the series every driver wants to reach.

➤ Nationwide: One step below the Sprint Cup. The cars are not as powerful and the races aren't as long.

➤ Craftsman Truck: Powerful racing versions of production pickup trucks give young drivers good training for the two higher series.

to your family and the rest of the general public. Oddly enough, they really are "stock" cars, in the true meaning of the word!

NASCAR has set up rules so that races are fair for every driver. Beginning in 2008, each car must now have the same basic body design, engine size, tires, and other parts. Officially, it's called the Car of Tomorrow—or *COT*, for short. Whether it's an Impala, Charger, Fusion, or Camry, every car must still follow COT rules.

Let's meet the COT, starting from the outside, called the *shell* or *body*. It's made of steel, which is carefully shaped to safely handle high speeds. How air moves over, under, and around the race car at high speeds is called *aerodynamics*.

Here's an easy way to show how aerodynamics works. Next time you're riding your bike, hold out one

The Car of Tomorrow features a wing on top of the deck lid (the NASCAR word for the trunk area). The wing helps keep the car under control at high speeds.

9

hand and point your fingers to the sky, with your palm facing forward. You'll feel the air "push" back. Then point your fingers straight ahead and feel the air move more easily over your hand. You've just improved the aerodynamics of your hand!

To improve the COT's aerodynamics, there are *roof flaps* at the back of the roof. There is also a *rear spoiler* at the back end of the car. The spoiler is a metal blade attached to the *deck lid*, NASCAR slang for the trunk door. The flaps and spoiler help the car's rear tires get **traction**, or grip firmly to the track at high speeds.

If you think of the body as the COT's skin, the *chassis* is the steel skeleton. The chassis supports the body, engine, wheels, and other parts of the car.

Dale Earnhardt Jr. puts on a HANS device. The black-and-red collar goes over his shoulders. The straps attached to the helmet are there to keep his head still.

The *cockpit* is the where the driver sits. It is surrounded by a *roll cage*—thick steel tubing that protects the driver in case the car flips or rolls over in an accident.

The cockpit of the COT is nothing like the inside of your car! There's no radio or CD player, no air-conditioning or heat, and just a single seat for the driver. The driver wears special seat belts, plus a *HANS Device*. That stands for Head and Neck Support System.

Strapped safely in the cockpit, the driver keeps a sharp eye on several *gauges* that show how the car's running, especially the engine. There's also a switch to shut the engine off in an emergency, a fire extinguisher, and a radio button on the steering wheel.

Here are the most important engine parts:

➤ *Carburetor*—Controls gas going from the *fuel cell* (a special gas tank) to the engine.

➤ *Cylinder*—One of eight metal tubes inside the engine in which a *piston* moves up and down to turn the . . .

➤ *Crankshaft*—Rotating rod connected first to the pistons. It turns to spin the . . .

➤ *Driveshaft*—Long rotating rod connected to the rear axle. The driveshaft turns the axle, which then turns the rear wheels. Vroom!

Track Terms

NOW THAT YOU CAN TALK THE TALK ABOUT
the not-so-stock cars that star in NASCAR, it's time
to take them to the track. There are hundreds of
racetracks across the country, in small towns and big
cities. Some are old-fashioned, oval dirt tracks, 1/4 of a
mile (.4 km) or less in length. Then there are modern
superspeedways, such as the 2.5-mile (4 km) Daytona
International Speedway.

   Each track has its own personality that makes it
unique. Maybe it's a tricky turn, or a wide straightaway,
or even a concession stand where they serve great local
barbecue. But all 22 tracks where NASCAR runs its Sprint
Cup races share a common language.

   Let's start by learning about the four types of tracks
where Sprint Cup races are run:

[OPPOSITE]
*The famous Bristol
Motor Speedway in
Tennessee is a good
example of a "short"
track. It's only a little
more than a half-mile
(.8 km) around.*

   1) Short: An oval that is less than one mile (1.6 km)
   in length. Expect plenty of bumping and banging
   as drivers try to pass on the tight curves. Example:
   Bristol Motor Speedway, Bristol, Tennessee; .533
   miles (.86 km) long.

   2) Intermediate: An oval that is greater than one mile
   (1.6 km) in length, but less than 2 miles (3.2 km)
   long. Not too short and not too long, these tracks are

TRACK TRIVIA

OLDEST
**Martinsville
Speedway,
Martinsville, Virginia
First race:
Sept. 25, 1949**

NEWEST
**Kansas Speedway,
Kansas City, Kansas
First race:
Sept. 30, 2001**

LONGEST
**Talladega
Superspeedway,
2.66 miles (4.28 km)**

SHORTEST
**Martinsville
Speedway,
Martinsville, Virginia
.526 miles (.85 km)**

MOST BANKING
**Talladega
Superspeedway,
33 degrees**

just right for a mixture of speed, braking, and turning. Example: Darlington Raceway, Darlington, South Carolina; 1.366 miles (2.2 km) long.

3) Superspeedway: A track that is greater than two miles (3.2 km) in length. Drivers can go so fast on the long straightaways, at two of these tracks NASCAR requires a special engine device, called a *restrictor plate*, which limits speeds. Example: Talladega Superspeedway, Talladega, Alabama; 2.66 miles (4.28 km) long.

4) Road Course: Road courses are not clean ovals, but odd-shaped routes, with straightaways and twisty "S" curves, which means drivers make left- and right-hand turns. Example: Watkins Glen International, Watkins Glen, New York; 2.45 miles (3.94 km) long.

Before exploring some unusual things about individual racetracks, you should be familiar with common terms used at each one. *Straightaway* means a long, straight stretch of track. Cars go fastest on straightaways. *Turns* are basic, as well, although some tracks have more than others. And drivers have to slow down depending on how sharp the turn is.

Banking in NASCAR-speak has nothing to do with the money a driver makes for winning a single race (2007

NASCAR champion Jimmie Johnson earned $415,386 for winning the UAW-DaimlerChrysler 400 that year!). Turns on many tracks have **banks**, which are areas that slope downward. Banking helps drivers maintain speed in turns. Some banks are steeper than others. The banking begins early in the turns, and then starts to flatten out as the turn finishes and the drivers speed up.

A concrete *wall* surrounds the outside of the track. NASCAR recently added *SAFER barriers*, or walls, at every track. SAFER stands for Steel and Foam Energy Reduction. The barrier, about 30 inches (76 cm) thick, is a combination of steel tubes and thick foam blocks that soften the **impact** when a car hits it. To understand how

This photo from Talladega shows how the turns at big tracks are tilted so drivers and their cars are "leaning" as they go through turns.

this might help a crashing car, imagine having a giant mattress to break your fall onto a concrete floor.

The inside edge of the track is called the *apron*. Then comes the *infield*, which is the large area in the center of the track. Every track has an infield, yet each one is set up differently. There are usually parking areas for cars and *recreational vehicles*, the enormous motor homes known as *RVs*. Die-hard NASCAR fans are famous for arriving in fancy RVs and camping in the infield for days. Many drivers and their families also travel to and from races in RVs. The sections of infields where they park become temporary driver villages.

The typical infield includes the *garages* where drivers' teams work on their race cars. Nearby are the drivers' 18-wheel *haulers*, giant tractor-trailer trucks that carry cars, engines, tools, and other necessary gear from race to race.

Alongside one of the straightaways is *pit road*. During a Sprint Cup race, each of the 43 drivers is assigned a *pit stall*, a space along pit road where cars are serviced during *pit stops* by *pit crews* (learn about what goes on in the pits in Chapters 3 and 4).

Most fans sit in *grandstands* behind the straightaway where the *start/finish line* is located. That section of the track also includes *concession stands* where food and beverages, programs, and souvenirs are sold. At the top

TRACK NICKNAMES

BRISTOL:
"The World's Fastest Half-Mile"
(One lap takes about 15 seconds!)

DARLINGTON:
"The Track Too Tough to Tame"

DOVER:
"Monster Mile"

INDIANAPOLIS:
"The Brickyard"
(The track used to be paved with bricks.)

Fans know that RVs make perfect viewing platforms once the race starts.

level are *private suites* (or *luxury boxes*) for fans and the *press section* for TV, radio, and other media.

Now that Car Talk and Track Terms are in your NASCAR vocabulary, get ready to put it all together on Race Day.

Pre-race Chatter

YOUR NASCAR LANGUAGE LESSONS WOULDN'T

be complete without experiencing an actual Sprint Cup race. That's where all the car talk and track terms come together. Before the race itself, however, there's still plenty to be done.

There are 43 **competitors** at the start of every Sprint Cup race. But drivers can't just show up and race. First, they have to *qualify*. That means a driver must prove that his car is fast enough to compete with the others.

Most Sprint Cup races are held on Sundays. Qualifying takes place on Fridays. Usually, more than 43 drivers try to qualify. Therefore, not every one makes it. So the competition really begins during qualifying.

Each driver can run two qualifying laps, going as fast as he can. Officials measure the time it takes to complete one lap, not the car's speed. The fastest time wins the No. 1 *pole position* for the start of Sunday's race. At the starting line, cars line up two-by-two. The No. 1 *pole sitter* is on the inside (closest to the infield), with No. 2 beside him, and so on for all 43 cars. As in many types of races, being in the front is an advantage.

Before and after qualifying, drivers are allowed *practice* runs. That's when they can make changes to

[OPPOSITE]
Jimmie Johnson enjoys his spot as the "pole sitter" for a 2005 race in Chicago. Starting on the pole gives drivers a chance to get out to an early lead.

19

the car's engine and *suspension*, called its *setup*. The suspension is the system of springs, **shock absorbers**, and other parts connected to the wheels.

A car's setup affects its *handling* on the track. The handling is *tight* if the front tires lose traction before the rear tires do. A tight car doesn't seem able to steer sharply enough through turns. Instead, the front end continues toward the wall. The opposite of tight is *loose*. That's when the rear tires have trouble getting traction on curves and turns. That causes the car to *fishtail* as the rear end swings outward during turns.

The driver qualifies by driving alone. But then and on race day, he's not really solo. Let's meet the different NASCAR race team members and learn about their jobs. Although the driver gets the most attention, the team wouldn't exist without an *owner*. He or she is the person who buys the cars, engines, tires, and dozens of other things it takes to compete in Sprint Cup racing. The owner pays everyone's **salary**, too. Many owners have two or three separate cars and teams.

Running a single Sprint Cup team can cost between $10-20 million a year! The owner finds *sponsors*, which are companies that pay to have their **logos** on drivers' cars and uniforms. Sponsorship is a form of advertising. A company hopes that fans who root for a driver it sponsors will buy its products or services.

After practices, drivers get one more chance to make changes. That happens during a 60-minute period on Saturday known as "Happy Hour."

Every team has a main sponsor, whose logo is the largest on the car. Companies such as Kellogg's, M&Ms, Home Depot, FedEx, Burger King, and Target pay millions of dollars to have their logos seen by millions of fans at tracks and on TV. Teams also have several minor sponsors, who don't pay as much and whose logos are displayed smaller.

The boss of the team is the *crew chief*. He makes sure that everyone's doing their jobs and that the car is in top shape before and during races. He and the driver discuss how the car is handling and make plans for each race. Other members of the team include:

➤ *Fabricators:* They build the body of the car from sheet metal.

➤ *Engineers:* Highly trained and college-educated experts who work on the car's design, aerodynamics, engine, and setup.

➤ *Mechanics:* They are assigned to work on specific parts of the car, from the engine to the tires

➤ Seven members of the team do double-duty on race day as members of the *pit crew* (see box on page 23).

Lowe's is the main sponsor of Jimmie Johnson's team, but other companies pay to put smaller patches on his clothing.

On Sunday morning of race day, there's lots to do. The team wakes up early to go over last-minute preparations and make sure that everything is ready for the race. The driver chats with the media, fans, and sponsors, and probably eats a meal.

Two hours before the race starts, all 43 drivers and their crew chiefs must attend an official NASCAR meeting. Every car must also pass a final technical *inspection* in the garage area. Inspectors check the car's weight, height, engine, safety equipment, and body to be sure NASCAR rules are obeyed.

NASCAR race machines are not driven out to the track . . . they're pushed by the crew. It takes a few guys to move this massive beast!

Meet the Pit Crew

Seven members of the team make up the pit crew. Each one has a specific job during a fast-and-furious pit stop.

➤ *Jack man:* Uses a 20-pound (9-kg) jack to lift one side of the car off the ground, just high enough so worn tires (including metal wheels) can be changed. Lifts and lowers one side at a time.

➤ *Rear tire changer:* Working on one rear tire at a time, he loosens five round metal pieces, called *lug nuts,* that hold the tire to the rear axle. Removes the tires, replaces them with new ones, and tightens the lug nuts.

➤ *Rear tire carrier:* Grabs worn tires from the rear tire changer and hands him new ones.

➤ *Front tire changer:* Removes and replaces both front tires.

➤ *Front tire carrier:* Assists the front tire changer.

➤ *Gas man:* Uses two 11-gallon (42-l) cans of gas (fuel) to fill the 17.75-gallon (67-l) fuel cell.

➤ *Catch-can man:* Holds a special container under the port (opening) where gas goes into the fuel cell to catch any overflow.

After a car gets the thumbs-up, the pit crew pushes it out to the team's pit stall. Drivers are introduced to the fans and climb into their cars. Then the track announcer gives auto racing's most famous command: "Gentlemen, start your engines!" The thunderous roar of 43 engines fills the air. The crowd goes crazy. Everyone's ready for the race to start.

Race Rap

IT'S "GO" TIME! THE CARS LINE UP, ACCORDING to their pole positions, behind the official *pace car*. The pace car slowly leads the pack around the track a few times. Finally, as they approach the start line, the pace cars pulls away. The *flag man*, on a stand high above the start/finish line, waves the *green flag* to begin the race.

Within seconds, the cars are going *flat out* (as fast as the weather and track conditions allow). Each driver immediately tries to find a *groove* on the track. That's slang for the best and fastest route around the track. Some drivers go for a *high groove*, which takes a car closer to the outside wall for most of a lap. Others prefer a *low groove*, which takes a car closer to the apron.

Before too long, a driver can feel how his car is handling. He talks about it on the car's radio with his crew chief, who stands on a platform overlooking the pit stall. If the car is either tight or loose, they'll decide how to adjust the setup during a pit stop. They discuss tire wear and gas, too.

The driver also keeps in radio contact with his *spotter*. The spotter sits high above the track, where he can see the entire field of cars. From there, he can tell the driver when to pass or when cars are going to pass him and warn him about crashes.

Drafting plays a huge role in NASCAR. Drafting is when one car runs just inches behind another, almost touching. The aerodynamics of the front car actually pulls the rear car, almost like a magnet. Because it's being pulled, the rear car doesn't use as much power and saves gas. Drafting cars go faster than they would separately. On longer tracks, cars form chains.

In the words of TV announcer Darrell Waltrip, "Boogity, boogity, boogity, let's get racin'!" However you say it, green means go on race day.

Time to slow down! The yellow flag means there has been an accident and all cars have to slow down to the same speed. The pace car (yellow, at far right) gets out in front to lead the cars on the caution laps.

Drafting sets up a tricky passing maneuver called a *slingshot pass*. Let's say one car is drafting behind another and wants to go ahead. The driver of the rear car pulls out from behind. That breaks the flow of air and shoots the rear car past the leader—like a slingshot.

With 43 cars going flat out at nearly 200 mph (322 kph), drafting and passing each other for up to 600 miles (966 km), things can get dangerous on the track. There are bound to be some cars bumping and rubbing against each other—or *trading paint* in NASCAR slang. If a driver isn't careful, a slight bump can send his car out of control and possibly crashing into other cars or the wall.

As tires wear, due to hot weather or a rough surface on the track, little bits of rubber break off. Those pieces are called *marbles* (or *loose stuff*). They collect on the upper part of the track near the wall, especially in curves and turns. Marbles can get slick and slippery and cause a car to lose control. If a car "goes into the marbles," the driver must be careful.

Crashes do happen in NASCAR. Safer cars and walls help prevent injuries, but the race is immediately slowed down when there's a crash. The flag man waves the *yellow flag*—yellow for caution—signaling drivers to slow down and stay in position in a single line behind the pace car. Once the track is cleared of any wrecked cars and debris, the green flag comes out again and the race resumes with every car still in the same position.

Pit stops are another major part of every race. A race can be won or lost depending on how well teams handle their pit stops. The difference between first place and second is often just a fraction of a second, so literally every second counts in NASCAR.

Teams try to plan how many pit stops to make during an entire race. Depending on the track and length of the race, the crew chief can calculate how many stops to make for gas and tires.

A normal pit stop is for gas and four new tires. Sometimes, to save precious seconds, a driver might make a *splash 'n' go* stop, just for gas. Or he might only change the two left-side tires (they wear quicker because of only making left turns).

A typical Sprint Cup race includes four to six pit stops. Most teams change tires and refuel during every one of these trips, which can take from 12-20 seconds each.

As the final laps wind down, the lead is seldom safe. There are usually a few cars trying to catch the leader. With one lap to go, the lead driver sees the *white flag* that signals his final lap. Now he really goes flat out. Sure enough, he's first under the *checkered flag*—which means he wins! After spinning a couple of celebration **doughnuts** on the infield grass, he heads for *Victory Lane* to get his trophy (the big paycheck comes later!).

That night, the car and tons of gear will be loaded into the hauler. Within a couple of days, the driver and rest of the team will be at the site of the next race. And the whole stock car racing routine will start over again.

Now that you've learned the colorful language of NASCAR, you know exactly what everyone's talking about.

Lots of drivers, like Kyle Busch here, celebrate victories by "doin' doughnuts." That's when they spin the tires so fast, the car turns in circles and the rubber burns up (creating lots of smoke).

Talkin' More NASCAR

Here are some other great NASCAR slang terms that didn't fit into the rest of our book:

Bear grease: Slang to describe any patching material used to fill cracks and holes or smooth bumps on a track's surface.

Blown motor: Major engine failure, usually ending a driver's day in a cloud of smoke and steam.

Chute: Slang for a straightaway.

Dirty air: Tricky air currents, caused by speeding cars, that can cause cars to lose control.

Dropping the rag: Slang for waving the green flag to start or restart a race.

Field: All the cars on a racetrack.

Ride: Slang for when a team hires a driver, as in "Dale Earnhart Jr. has a ride with Hendrick Motorsports."

Silly Season: Slang for the time, late in the race season, when news and rumors begin about teams changing drivers, crews, and/or sponsors for the following year.

Stick: Slang for tire traction, as in "the car's sticking to the track."

Stickers: Slang for new tires, complete with the manufacturer's sticker.

200-mph tape (or racer's tape): Duct tape strong enough to hold a banged up car together and finish a race.

Glossary

association a group of people or companies who are in a similar job or have similar interests

banks on a racetrack, the tilted sections of the roadway

competitors the people competing in a contest

doughnuts smoky, rubber-burning circles created by a NASCAR racer after a victory

impact hitting against something else

logos symbols that represent companies or teams

salary the money a person is paid to do a job

shock absorbers car parts that move up and down as the car goes around turns or over bumps, helping to create a smooth ride

technical having to do with technology, machinery, or engineering

traction the gripping power of something on a slippery or smooth surface

Find Out More

BOOKS

Eyewitness NASCAR
By James Buckley Jr.
DK Publishing, 2005
This photo-filled book takes you inside the world of NASCAR. See close-up pictures of engines and other gear, meet the heroes of the sport, and see more photos of pit-stop and racing action.

History of NASCAR
By Jim Francis
Crabtree Publishing, 2008
Take a trip back in time to see how NASCAR first roared onto the American sports scene.

NASCAR at the Track
By Mike Kennedy and Mark Stewart
Lerner Publishing, 2007
This book takes a close-up look at various NASCAR tracks, showing how they're designed, built, and how drivers attack each type of track.

NASCAR Record & Fact Book
Sporting News Books, 2008
Loaded with facts and figures about current drivers and NASCAR history, this handy reference source also includes a stock car racing glossary and pit-stop details.

Pit Pass
By Bob Woods
Readers' Digest Children's Publishing, 2005
Take an "inside" look at NASCAR tracks, drivers, cars, and gear.

WEB SITES

Visit our Web site for lots of links about NASCAR terms:
www.childsworld.com/links

Note to Parents, Teachers, and Librarians: We routinely check our Web links to make sure they're safe, active sites—so encourage your readers to check them out!

Index

accidents, 26, 27
aerodynamics, 9–10
apron, 16

banks and banking, 14–15
"The Brickyard", 16
Bristol Motor Speedway,
    13, 14, 16
Busch, Kyle, 28

car handling, 5, 20, 24
car manufacturers, 8, 9
Car of Tomorrow (COT),
    9–11
car parts, 5, 9–11, 20, 29
chassis, 10
cockpit, 11
costs, 20
Craftsman Truck, 8
crew chief, 21, 22, 24, 27

Darlington Raceway, 14, 16
doughnuts, 28
Dover Speedway, 16
drafting, 25–26

Earnhardt, Dale, Jr., 10
engine parts, 11

fan areas, 16–17
flags, 24, 26, 27, 28, 29
France, William "Big Bill", 8

garage, 16, 22
Gordon, Jeff, 5
groove, 24

HANS Device, 10, 11
hauler, 16, 28

infield, 16
inspection, pre-race, 22–23

Johnson, Jimmie, 15, 19, 21

Kansas Speedway, 14

marbles, 26–27
Martinsville Speedway, 14
media area, 17

NASCAR history, 7, 8
NASCAR rules, 9, 14,
    22–23
Nationwide, 8

pace car, 24
pit crew, 16, 21–22, 23
pit road, 16
pit stall, 16
pit stop, 3, 16, 23, 27
plate, restrictor, 14
pole position, 5, 19, 24
pre-race terms, 19–23
production models, 8–9

qualifying to compete, 5,
    19–20

race time, 5, 19, 24–28,
    29
recreational vehicles (RV),
    16, 17

roll cage, 11
roof flap, 10

setup, 20
speed, 26
spoiler, rear (wing), 9, 10
sponsors and logos, 20–21
spotter, 25
Sprint Cup, 8, 13, 19, 27
stock cars, 7–8
straightaway, 14

Talladega Superspeedway,
    14, 15
team members, 21–22,
    23, 25
tires, 26, 27, 29
track nicknames, 16
track surface, 27, 29
track terms, 13–17, 29
track trivia, 14
traction, 10
"tradin' paint", 5, 26
turns, 14

vehicles, support, 16, 17,
    28

walls and barriers, 15–16
Waltrip, Darrell, 25
Watkins Glen International,
    14

ABOUT THE AUTHOR

Bob Woods is a writer who lives in Connecticut. He has written many books and magazine articles about motor sports, and was the editor of the Harley-Davidson motorcycle company's 100th anniversary magazine.

WITHDRAWN FROM
HERRICK DISTRICT LIBRARY